Little Boy

Little Boy

alison mcghee AND peter h. reynolds

ATHENEUM BOOKS FOR YOUNG READERS   New York   London   Toronto   Sydney

Little boy, so much depends on . . .

your yellow cup,

a serenade to wake you up,

sun that slants across the rug,

the wings on that astonishing bug,

and...

your big cardboard box.

Little boy, so much depends on...

a puddle to jump,

sand to dump,

truck down the hall,

Little boy, so much depends on . . .

a blue mixing bowl,

a ball in the goal,

the tree that fell,

that wet-dog smell,

and...

your big cardboard box.

Little boy, so much depends on...
    animal crackers on the couch,

a Band-Aid for an ouch,

shoes that tie,

waving good-bye,

and...

your big cardboard box.

Little boy, so much depends on...
        Your starship pajamas,

that story about llamas,

the way you don't worry,

the way you won't hurry,

and...

your big cardboard

box.

Little boy, you remind me how
so much depends on days made of now.

*For Donald Hoffbeck McGhee, who
used to pull me up the hill on the
toboggan, with love and respect
—A. M.*

*To my father, Keith H. Reynolds,
whose light will always shine,
always guide
—P. H. R.*

Atheneum Books for Young Readers
An imprint of Simon & Schuster
Children's Publishing Division
1230 Avenue of the Americas
New York, New York 10020
Text copyright © 2008 by
Alison McGhee
Illustrations copyright © 2008 by
Peter H. Reynolds
Book design by Ann Bobco
The text for this book is handlettered.
The illustrations for this book are
rendered in pen, ink, and watercolor.
Manufactured in the United States of
America
First Edition
10 9 8 7 6 5 4 3 2 1
Library of Congress Cataloging-in-
Publication Data
McGhee, Alison, 1960–
Little boy / Alison McGhee ; illustrated by
Peter H. Reynolds. — 1st ed.
p.   cm.
Summary: A father reflects on how the
future depends upon all of the little
things in his son's world, from his yellow
drinking cup to a big cardboard box.
ISBN-13: 978-1-4169-5872-7
ISBN-10: 1-4169-5872-X
[1. Fathers and sons—Fiction.]
I. Reynolds, Peter H., 1961– ill. II. Title.
PZ7.M4784675Lit 2008
[E]—dc22
2007029625